No Longer Property of
EWU Libraries

Erica Silverman
Illustrated by S. D. Schindler

Macmillan Publishing Company New York
Maxwell Macmillan Canada Toronto
Maxwell Macmillan International New York Oxford Singapore Sydney

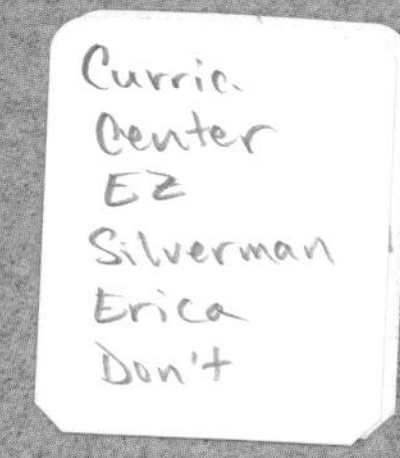

To Kofi and Leilani—true champions. —E. S.

 Macmillan Publishing Company is part of the Maxwell Communication Group of Companies. Macmillan Publishing Company, 866 Third Avenue, New York, NY 10022. Maxwell Macmillan Canada, Inc., 1200 Eglinton Avenue East, Suite 200, Don Mills, Ontario M3C 3N1. First edition. Printed in the United States of America. The text of this book is set in 16 pt. Aster. The illustrations are rendered in pastels on colored paper.
10 9 8 7 6 5 4 3 2 1

Library of Congress Cataloging-in-Publication Data
Silverman, Erica.
Don't fidget a feather! / Erica Silverman ; illustrated by S. D. Schindler. — 1st ed. p. cm. Summary: Their contest to decide who is the champion of champions almost has disastrous consequences for Gander and Duck.
ISBN 0-02-782685-6 [1. Competition (Psychology)—Fiction. 2. Ducks—Fiction. 3. Geese—Fiction.]
I. Schindler, S. D., ill. II. Title. PZ7.S58625Fr 1994 [E]—dc20 93-8707

One day, Duck went swimming in the lake. What a great swimmer I am, she thought.

Just then, she heard a big splash.
"Greetings, Duck," said Gander.
"Hi, Gander. Watch me swim." Duck paddled as fast as she could.
"Not bad," said Gander. "But I'm faster."

"Let's race," said Duck. "Ready...set...go!"
And off they swam across the lake.
Duck came in first. "Ta-dah! I am the champion."

"Maybe," said Gander. "But I can fly higher than you."

"Can not," said Duck.

Gander flapped his wings. "Ready…set…go!"

And up they flew above the spruce trees.

Gander flew higher. "I am the champion of champions."

"No, you aren't," said Duck.

"Yes, I am," said Gander.

Thud. Thump. They landed side by side.

Duck fluffed out her feathers. She waddled back and forth.

Finally, she turned to Gander. "Let's have a freeze-in-place contest," she said. "Don't move. Don't talk. Don't fidget a feather! And the winner will be the one and only, true and forever champion of champions."

"That's me," said Gander.

"We'll see," said Duck. "Ready...set...freeze!"

Gander stood still. So did Duck. She watched Gander. She waited for him to move.

A bee flew out of the bushes. *Bzzzzz.* It zigged around Gander's head. *Bzzzzz.* It zagged around his tail.

It won't be long, thought Duck, before I will be the one and only, true and forever champion of champions.

But Gander did not move.

The bee zigzagged toward Duck. *Bzzzzz*. It hovered over her head. *Bzzzzz*. It landed on her neck.

Duck did not move one muscle. She did not quack one quack. She did not fidget one feather.

The bee flew away.

Duck waited and waited for Gander to move.

A horde of bunnies bounded over. They perched on Gander's head. They slid down his long neck.

Soon, thought Duck, soon I will be the one and only, true and forever champion of champions.

But Gander did not move.

The bunnies surrounded Duck. They tapped on her beak. They played with her webbed feet. They leapfrogged across her back.

Duck did not move one muscle. She did not quack one quack. She did not fidget one feather.

At last, the bunnies hopped away.

Duck waited and waited and waited for Gander to move.

Caw, caw, caw. A cluster of crows swooped down.

They circled around Gander's head. They landed on Gander's back. They bounced up and down.

Any second now, thought Duck, I will be the one and only, true and forever champion of champions.

But Gander did not move.

The crows swarmed around Duck. They fluttered their wings in her face. They cawed in her ears. They tickled her tail feathers.

Duck did not move one muscle. She did not quack one quack. She did not fidget one feather.

Caw, caw, caw. The crows flew away.

A sudden wind gusted up. Clouds of dust rose into the air. Branches swayed and leaves scattered.

Whooosh! The wind blew Gander into a grove of dandelions.

Whoooosh! It knocked Duck into a mulberry bush.

After a long, long time, the wind settled down to a sighing breeze.

Half a second more, thought Duck, and—

Along came Fox.

"What luck!" Fox's nose quivered with delight. "Dinner tonight and dinner tomorrow! Dinner just waiting to be cooked!"

Out of the corner of her eye, Duck could see Gander.

Gander did not move.

Then neither will I, thought Duck.

Fox rolled Duck and Gander into his sack and fastened it tight.

Then he dragged and pushed and pulled it through the woods.

Fox took Duck and Gander out and set them down next to each other. He started a big pot of water boiling. He chopped up potatoes, tomatoes, carrots, celery, and squash. He threw in a handful of beans. He added garlic and pepper. He stirred the stew.

Then he turned and looked at Gander.
Gander did not move one muscle. He did not quack one quack. He did not fidget one feather.
Neither did Duck.
Eyes sparkling, Fox pointed from one to the other.

"Eeny meeny miny mander.
Cook a duck or cook a gander?
My tummy says to pick this one,
and that is Y-O-U."

Fox carried Gander over to the pot.

Gander has to move now, thought Duck.

But Gander did not.

Fox opened the lid. Clouds of hot steam billowed out.

Move, Gander. Please move, thought Duck.

But Gander did not.

What if Gander can't move? thought Duck. What if he's too afraid?

Fox lifted Gander high. "In we go."

"*Quaccckkk!* Don't cook my friend!" Duck snapped at Fox's tail. She nipped at his nose.

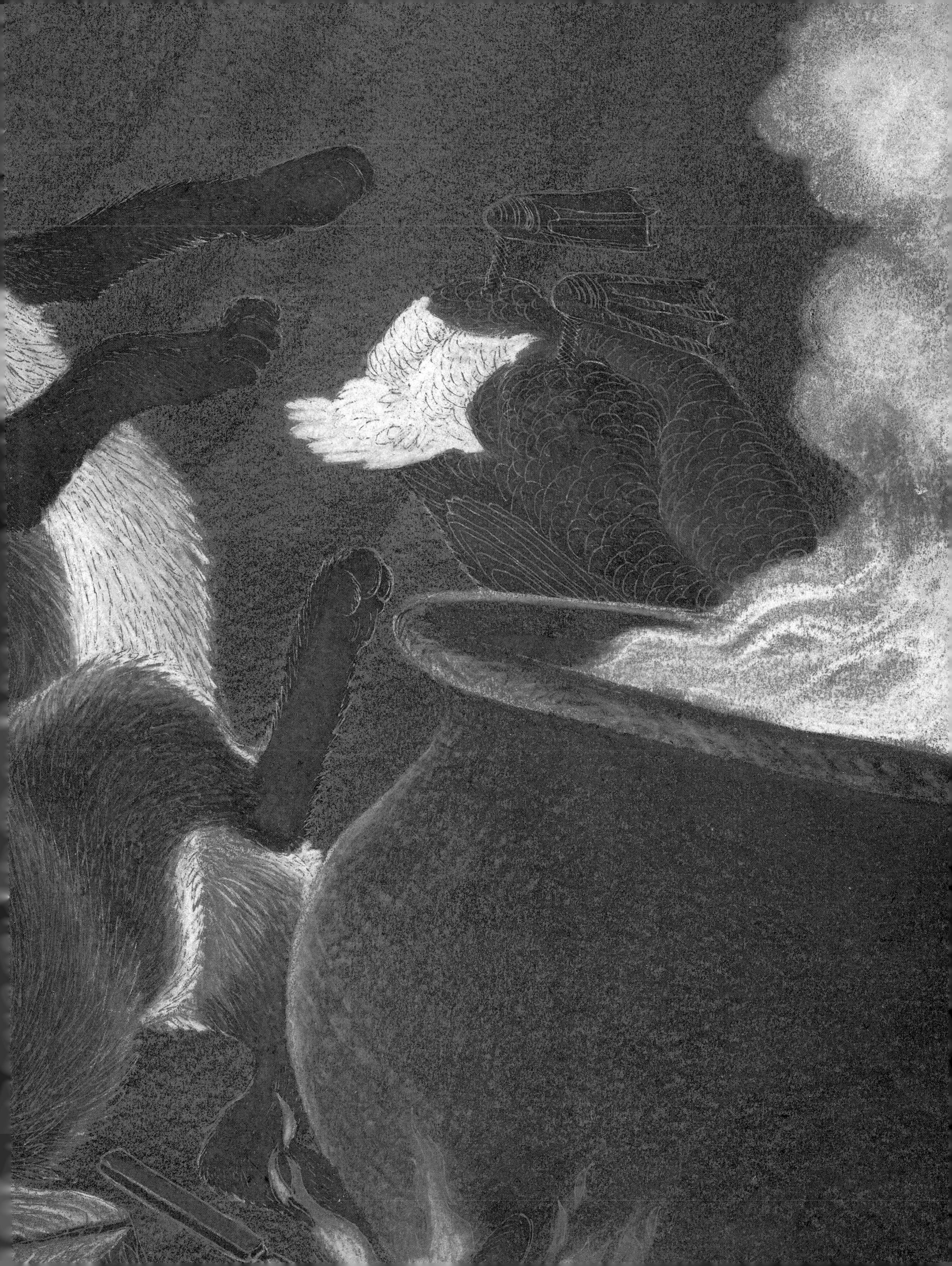

"Help! Help!" Fox dropped Gander and went running off into the woods.

Duck and Gander watched him go.

Duck sighed. "Well, Gander, I guess you win the freeze-in-place contest."

"Maybe," said Gander. "But, you, Duck, are the one and only, true and forever champion of champions."

"I am?" Duck stared at Gander. Then she smiled and puffed out her feathers. "Yes. I suppose I am."

Gander peeked into the pot. "Smells good. Shall we eat?"

And they ate the whole pot of Fox's delicious vegetable stew.